Kelsey!

May the wo

inspire, ignite anc

your journey!

MW00721319

Egregorial Annunciation

JAMES FYRE

INFINITY PUBLISHING

Copyright © 2012 by James Fyre

ISBN 978-0-7414-7709-5 Hardcover
ISBN 978-0-7414-7710-1 eBook
Library of Congress Control Number: 2012941010

Printed in the United States of America

Published August 2012

INFINITY PUBLISHING
1094 New DeHaven Street, Suite 100
West Conshohocken, PA 19428-2713
Toll-free (877) BUY BOOK
Local Phone (610) 941-9999
Fax (610) 941-9959
Info@buybooksontheweb.com
www.buybooksontheweb.com

TABLE OF CONTENTS

A Thousand Faces

Awoke with lidless filmy orbs for eyes,
A mirrored room did loom—the self-despise.
Her reflection a thousand faces feared,
Horrific repetition realized.
Realities soft voices within seared,
Her endless catacomb her home—she sneered.
> Bereaved of passed pseudo pretense of soul,
> For sight of Self revealed herself—a whole.
> Her images of pious perspective,
> Subjected under consequence control.
> Release the pain of mind within forgive,
> Her image, beauty's visage—willed to live.
She caught a glimpse, of her reflections pure,
She only knew, that few, could touch—such cure.

Seduction Pools

Pulled down, beneath the undertow
"No vacancy" labeled mind.
The seas dunes shift wildly,
And then,
Bleak blackened wells
Peer past focus.
Mooned light, accentuates
This stark shuddering sight.
Visage fair, picturesque
Pearl night-shadowed hair.
Surely, princess ancestry
Formed Victorian beauty.
The Artist's ideal
This canvas turned flesh,
Innocent seductress,
Entangled now in her spell.
Drowning,
Onerous oxygen,
Lungs perspire,
Startled, shocked
A beauteous betrayal.

And then,
Pools of darkness
Awoke this sudden slumber
Resurfaced, thrown to the shore.
Conscious, alive
Twin circling shadows
Soak in one desire.
Overcome this will to fall
Into these pools of seduction,

I enter,
And then...

Despairing Beast

The wilderness was deserted as an ancient tomb,
Desolate and futile, like an empty barren womb.
This, the land of the despairing beast,
Absent even, were leaves on which to feast.

Returning to the firmament of extinguished life,
Their fate was damned to dust, a fate proved rife.
To be alive was to be alone,
To wander helplessly on your own.

Life in constant waves of decay began to deteriorate,
The beast's body leisurely stiffened as it began to macerate.
Nevermore would it roam and linger,
It was left to gorge itself in inhumane hunger.

Life was finite, death came in the cool of night,
Beast's lay decaying in the mornings brooding light.
Life's stubborn cycle ceased to repeat,
As the beast's existence did deplete.

Eternity a fallacy for the primitive world,
Dying as it must, in dust it shaped a new mold.
Forever they lie under man's foot,
Body's decrepitly turned to dirt and soot.

Despair accompanied death as it scoured the land,
Never knowing when fate would lead one by the hand.
Down to the depths of grit and ground,
To rot under layers of earth and mound.

Life and death, a wheel of fate's holistic pattern,
This life of hedonistic ideals would never discern.
The beast's simple pleasures quickened death,
Until the last beast breathed it's last breath.

Shadow Maker

Blanketed in a void of black, I can't breathe,
Dark wings surround my living sphere.
Confused into delusion,
In the mezzanine I stand,
All alone.

To be free of me, utter impossibility,
I coil myself in my own deceit.
Created my horror,
In the shadows I hide,
All alone.

The door is shut, prevents my escape,
The shadows creep, into my soul.
Weeping for release,
In the abyss I fall,
All alone.

Coveting joy as it passes by,
This conscious my own creation, I must abide.
Misfit of truth,
In the darkness I exhale,
All alone.

The pressure overbearing, life overturns,
My life's in dis-ease with no known cure.
Dying from guilt,
In the sandstone I die,
All alone.

Beauty's Demise

Vanishing valleys disappear at nights
      last lights.
Miserably mist settles amongst the curtains
      of mountains.
Sky's silhouette starstruck protruding peaks of stark
      ghostly grandeur.
Awaiting waking sun, to ambush from blue black,
      dawn's swift.

Still sitting in wait for the sun's first sight
      after night.
Clearing clouds off mischievous snow-caps,
      mountainous traps.
Heavenly heat beats upon the cliffs'
      sweating rocks.
While watching for the weeping rivers
      wailing doom.

Tempered trees do expiate as gloom
      does deliver
Its intolerable vow to time's clocks
      fickle riffs.
Yet yonder your serene beautiful scene,
      things unseen
Fire furious furnaces, liquid magma flows,
      Stone sows.

Deviant discretion of too subtle a gift
      will crack.
Blatant becomes nature's dreary murderer,
      the dark.
Her hallowed rays of furnished gold
      do hold.
Until unaware of nights creeping frown,
      sun's down.

An Earthly Angel

She swiftly flew above the scattered clouds,
Along strewn isles, begot sea-salted eyes,
She shook her wings off, living with the crowds,
Searching her heart, she heard the lover's cries.
She humbly left her place, in the heav'nly host,
Her yearning brought her to passions desire,
She, heaven sent, led by the holy ghost,
Revealed to her a man she would admire.
She was an angel, who followed her heart,
In having to choose, life on earth, her choice,
The tears fell, she had forgotten her part,
Her hands gave love, and heaven held her voice.
      To live as mortal in the arms of man,
      The hosts of angels, how they understand.

The Egregore

I.

Unconscious thoughts intertwine
Amidst misplaced memories
Within vivid dreams
A rectified reality

The bloom of immortality
Crawled from the grave
Freed of the pit
Sanctum Sheol

From dust dried
Breath made flesh
Blank slate born
Chaste womb delivered

Perished Persistence

The wind to hot, his orifice too swollen to swallow,
As if constricted by stagnant air,
Air that's heavy, wretched, yet fair.
His body lay grafted to the gritty resting fallow.
Left to wander the wonders of the desert,
To travel fate bound—joy a whim—
Dust and dust confide in him.
Abandoned by suppressed souls, that tried to convert.
This hell his last haven, alone he resides in pain,
Away from the worldly hate,
Away from what they tried to create.
He strays in circles, his footprints come round again.
Uncaring to the peril ahead, he strode without fault,
Deeper into the vast barren sea,
The threats unconscious, he still free.
His mind torn with thought; his brain a spiraling vault.
Reservedly he ventured on, from dusk till dawn,
He persevered in pain and torment,
Tried to break free but tied in confinement.
His will his enemy, his mind his bodies brawn.
Ripped, his clothes clung to his scarlet-stained skin,
Battered shreds, a loin left to clasp,
The last piece of dignity he could grasp.
Shod with bare calluses, blistering sores grown in.
His finite journey had only begun to grow slow,
When lingering so close, yet, distant,
She slew him a smile in an inimical instant.
His memories malevolently charmed his disfigured glow.
Unwillingly his thoughts conjured the pain he felt,
Choking on his hate, he groped,
The sand his keeper, his conscious hoped.
His flaked parched skin, tormented by heat, began to melt.
There was no time to realize what he had become,
Overcome by knowledge's temptation,
Left to deplete in sorrowful contemplation.
Wondering how he manipulated his mind to succumb.

His thoughts corrupted his beautiful subconscious,
To control it, was an endless walk,
Catching bleak faces which can't talk.
In the confines of this mind, insanity was his conscious.

Lilith

Invoked entities feast
On this prone prospect
A flesh suit on strings
With a will to appease
The gesture of his dear
Lilith
Provoked to lead lives
On a path of seduction
For her inimical intent
Fates fumble and forget
The demise that befell
Lilith
Now she walks her prey
On a collar of indifference
To betray mislead honor
Shackled leashes bound
Around the subjects of
Lilith
Accustom now to her will
Belied still a life undone
A stricken heart compelled
In her beauteous shroud
One last wish to kill
Lilith
One with the ancient lust
Enthralled soul now rapt
By fallen succubus mistress
Depths unfathomable dwells
The untouchable shadows of
Lilith

Fallen

Disfigured innocence she bought,
    Was paid for with wanton thought.
She could not afford the price of life,
    When life not, but sorrow caught.

Disturbed of what she chose,
Knowing the darkness died, fought
For reasons which the thoughts now froze
By cyclic ways the villain shows.

Disgruntled confusion full of strife,
Fell she did, mankind's wife—
Naked and empty with no clothes—
Pain not pardoned, divorced was life.

Disgraced kingdom now wanes bare,
    For without relent was evils eyes stare.
No hope left, remorse knows no care,
    The now mortal, and surviving pair.

Blanket

Surrounded in sublime warmth, I disguise myself,
I'm a ghost, I'm a hero—
Quiet, sleeplessness keeps me awake.
Peace, keeps my mind from trouble—
Just another mask I hope to wear,
I'm invisible, I'm invincible—
Cuddling, clutching tender softness.
Shaking, stopped by gentle breeze—
Cherished it's kept, a loving memory,
I'm a child, I'm a man—
Stories, etched in each stain.
Time, rips through loved layers—
Wrapped in heat, awoke in sweat,
I've cried, I've screamed—
Changed, aged it may seem.
Endured, still lingering on.

Times Mime

Abeyant becomes death, when faced by time,
Infertile is its futile effort; brought
By Deaths desire to coin times mimicked mime,
To conspire, too condone what's heav'nly wrought.
Until Death knows it's but a fragment lost
In times long lawless eternal circle;
T'will dwell between an animistic cost,
Undone and impotent in fates cycle.
As death is held in heartless Hades' hands,
The present time begins to dissipate,
And then, when death affects souls, still time stands,
Opaquely constant, ensuring deaths fate.
      So, Death is dead, surpassed by timelessness,
      This end, an end, time rests in sleeplessness.

Refined

Clinging cloaks of ashen black,
Patient apparitions partook
Notoriously without weakness.
Snuffed light, utter darkness.
"Let loose", I slithered and shook,
Grinding grasp, my body cracked.

Progressive pain, till senses severed—
Can't think, thoughts constant provoke.
Father Time is dreaming,
Time stops it's ticking—
Awoke, awaiting air I choke,
Strapped, stunned, limbs delivered.

Platter, a plate, my fate is fear.
Tired torture leaves me limbless,
Useless piece of rotting flesh,
I ponder upon future quest.
Still immobile, left lifeless—
Extracted emotions, even tears.

Stunted spoon gouges, gashes
Out my eyes, quenched conscious—
Out of space, out of time,
Can't believe this pain is mine—
Speaking sputtered blood gushes
Tongue removed, rampant slashes.

Ears implode, life an infant memory,
Yet I live, my sin forgiven.
My body, burned parts,
Graciously given a new start.
Chance created, life lived.
Frozen flesh, body held heavenly.

Hellish haven, humanity revoked,

Torn, ripped to pieces,
Each piece a part of sin.
Flesh furnished, refined within.
Newly sown, heaven's choices.
Newly named, kingly cloaked.

II.

Forgotten choices
Recollect veritas past
Four-square paths
Karmic certain destiny

Winnowing wind
Refine these souls
Of bestial indifference
Genuflect god of love

Coalesced consciousness
Realign Mind divine
Too lights source
Truth's quarters

The Four Horsemen

"Come!" I stood, tall and proud, awaiting the Lord's command.
From his will, he hands me a bow to conquer the lands.
A crown of gods on my hcad, a steed of white under my feet,
A quarter of the world I've been released to defeat.
Bent on conquest, I strive for the cries of pleading men,
I feed on their ignorance, throats bellowing to live again.
Their woes my power; their sin my strength. My home
Lies within the bleeding hearts I've claimed mine own.
My arrows fly true, they pierce through man's hollow hide,
And to a house of slaughter I'll lead my dead tribe.

Deep scarlet tainted my blood stained stallion,
To war, long sword in hand, followed by a hellish battalion,
To abduct peace from the world, to put in place fear,
I was sent to turn man's hope to despair, to dry up feeble tears.
My name bloodshed, my purpose war, by my hand
Men slay each other, returning bodies back to dust and sand.
Turning hearts to stone, touching lips with hate,
Swaying men to mutilate, to meet at hell's gate.
The massacre quick, souls hasten to Hades lairs,
Never will these dead men ascend Heaven's stairs.

My darkness quenches the light sent from savored souls,
As these scales deliver disease through mans mucus holes.
I weigh the morsels that I take away, in these claws of malice
The grip of mans hunger withers subject to hell's devices.
Life giving grain is mine to ration to each convulsing intestine,
My brooding blackness inflicts dreaded maceration, I find divine.
I've dried up rich soil, embedded thorns and grafted decay,
And in reply to the sufferings of sin, I restrain growths delay.
This famine and drought make men forlorn, too weak in mind

To hope for deliverance from this constant ailment I've
refined.

As Sheol's spawn, I've awoken and heard deathly groans,
Now, I, Death, so pale and cold arise to turn flesh to bone.
To extinguish a quarter of men, to reopen the ever vacant
void
That awaits the souls I've damned by famine, plague and
sword.
The tiger, lion, behemoth and leviathan now obey my will,
Sent to devour the delicacy of man, until they've had their
fill.
This walking corpse, that reeks of hate and death
Has made man subject to transient horror without breath.
The gates are wide and welcome my new breed,
Forever will this dead multitude satisfy my voracious greed?

Jesus' Fate

My fate was known before this life began,
My choice to live, outside my will.
This heart is barren; this mind, empty.
This futile war must go on, until
The will of god is satisfied.
Until his son, the Lord does kill.

This turmoil I brought upon myself,
To suffer in anguish, yet have humility?
Are my cries a voice, lost in heaven's hymns?
"Eloi, Eloi, lama sabachthani?"
I seek my hope in my despair.
Yet by hell, I'll be free?

Purposes grow fragile when hell sneers
When the shadows conjure hate,
When the demons dance dauntingly,
The conscious fades to a haunting state.
The bread of life now begins to mold,
As the face of god ensures my fate.

My forsaken being nailed naked to a tree,
In humanities shame I welcomed hell.
I alone, the only one left to forgive,
The mass of ignorance under Satan's spell.
Spawned from the worlds sin,
To my burning abode my soul fell.

Torn, ripped, the curtain split,
Justice sentenced god's wrath upon my head.
Heavenly creatures despised the defeat—
Fallen angels from our sins are fed.
In daddy's hands my being, was held,
Now the devil pets my bloody head instead.

Lucifer's Prize

Long, long have I awaited such times,
While light begins to fade, as heaven weeps
For their pride, being beaten in his prime.
My minions of death summoned, creep
To the reality of the breathing,
They relish the angels seething.

Forever, this life bound to mine,
Fateful dooms infringe his thought,
Incestuous hate begins to malign
Inside the mind too long I've sought.
Now, my hellions arise,
It's time to slay our prize.

Impaled for all in this sordid hour,
Deserted to die, to die alone.
Abandoned by heaven, my morsel to devour.
His spirit diminished, left, his skin and bone.
His life severed by death,
Never to breathe a living breath.

Masquerade as an angel they've said,
I've been turned into an imaginary figment.
Now I laugh, god's beloved son is dead,
Now the deceived begin the lament.
All in vain, he's in my domain,
His spirit tormented, his body slain.

My gates of hell have entrapped
The spirit of 'Christ' from the lost,
Man's innocence, I now have raped,
Never again will the devil be crossed.
My power lies within hate,
I own all man's fate.

Damned Souls

A blood battle between forsaken kin,
Souls stole enduring in the underworld,
Destined to perdition alike they wait,
They wait while one kills another,
They wait to taste the blood of a brother.
Such vampires and lycan,
Rage,
Rage in the twilight
Of the night.
Thoughtless murder, a will to kill,
Purpose frail as blood beckons,
Fateful fangs deal justice fallen.
Pure,
Pure is union blood,
A concocted vile of deformity,
A mixture of two races,
A finality to minuscule discrepancy,
Two in one.
Blood,
For blood,
Fate,
For fate,
So ends the blood battle,
Between forsaken kin,
When kin unite,
The war's within.

Self Distortion

You forget the past,
    Relish the present,
        Delay the unknown.
You release your soul,
    Savor your spirit,
        Corrupt your thought.
You've deprived your body of life giving food,
I've given you temptation to change your mood.

I enjoy the sorrow,
    Share the suffering,
        Encourage the naught.
I take your freedom,
    Shatter your memories,
        Hear your groan.
I've distorted your image of conscious reality,
You've accepted your own sadistic frailty.

Lost in yourself,
You live out your pain,
Found what you searched for,
Now your fading in vain.

Revision

I've delivered disease within troubled minds,
I've confused their emotions with trackless thoughts,
  Hail!
He witnessed willing souls reconciled, fade away,
He released his freedom into hands of authority,
  Hail!
She boarded the vessel of the damned,
She disregarded truth and her proof of sanctity.
  Hail!
We've relinquished our grasp of humanity,
We've devised our own demise,
  Hail!
You absorb the wish of the master,
You believe the source of your existence,
  Hail!
I control man's disruptive corrupted mind,
I write the tapestries of life,
  Hail!

III.

Annunciate
In silenced numina
Threads weave
Presence perceived

Noble intention
Embrace eleven
Intuition nurtured
Even immersion

Ethereal existence
Astral alias submerge
Beyond conditional nature
Of sleeping sons

Miss Venom

She flauntingly struts through gutters of spite,
She ensnares her victims with little whites lies,
She steals innocence from oblivious blind men,
She deals fallen justice the Queen of the flies.
She, an angel of light, a venomous temptress,
She sows repressed hate uprooting her demise,
She has the traits of a promiscuous succubus,
She suppresses her fate but cannot disguise.

Away with her,
        The worlds her domain,
Evil she summons,
        The taste of disdain.
Her influence eternal,
        The words will remain,
Thieving lost souls,
        The witch must reign.

He gave her the strength to keep up the fight,
He told her her ways, were always right,
He said, "I love you forever,"
He stole her soul with pleasure.
He turned the day into night,
He took away her fading light,
He threw her rigid body to the fire,
He gave her an eternity to perspire.

There she waits,
        Left dying all alone,
Forever is infinite,
        Nobody hears her groan.
The darkness comfort,
        Only sound her moan,
Brooding loved fear,
        Mercy no never shown.

Fate

Incomprehensible strategy,
A devilish tragedy.
Fear of rejection,
Sufferings binding friction,
Inescapable is affliction.

"What's on the other side?
Can't think, have to hide."

Superficial mask,
Too painful a task.
Few choices, samsara awaits,
Shunned at, heavens gates,
Torment, is your eternal fate.

"Not my fault, he lied!
Too many tears I've cried."

Constant blame,
An impossible game.
Playing pieces, powers pawns,
Endless night, forgotten dawn,
Now lifeless, not remembered, ever gone.

"Life too long denied,
This body exhaled, died."

Children of the Watcher

Children of the heaven
Pursue flesh feminine
Lust after comely kin
Mimi-cry of the raven
Silent watcher spawn
Enamor celestial fawn
Woman angelic haven

      Enchantments charm
      Chiefs of tens mayhem
      Intrigued agreed condemn
      Semjaza foresee the harm
      Specie concoction phenom
      Spirit raged napalm
      Upon the shadowed smarm.

            Beget giants three thousand ells
            Ravish lands doomed soul
            Grigori fate darkened Sheol
            Devoured kin beneath caved hell
            Their souls await white-throned hall
            Fiery lake consumed their fall
            Dimension desert watcher's dwell

                  Azazels twilit sighted shelter
                  Seventy generations bore
                  Forlorn left woman whore
                  Children of the slaughter
                  Turned away feeble prayer
                  Faultless angelic affair
                  Children of the watcher

Steadfast

Frustrated inside,
    Living lies.
Hope dwindles,
    It fades,
    A false reality.
My dreams,
    Set aside.
Where's God?
    Steadfast still,
    Frailty undone.
I stand,
    Before gates.
The answer,
    Dwells inside,
    Unspoken humility.

One Faithful Prayer

Power with unknown time,
Impossible to express with mortal words.
Moved, our heart can only be,
It takes more than eyes to truly see.

Be open, and be made complete,
Obey and be marveled at truth.
Bask within his beautiful desire,
No more fear, no more scorching fire.

Not just a selfish plea for mercy,
Just a fellowship of two lifelong friends.
Deeper we grow inside the heart,
Until we see and know every part.

One word and all is shown,
A truth we can all know.
Men by a thought are healed,
Many visions and dreams revealed.

The river of splendor flows,
The fire of salvation burns,
Through the name that frees us,
That precious name of Jesus.

Mythical Creature

The essence of your virtues seizes hearts,
Your mythical beauty bewilders men;
Of this nature I find you hold a part
Of my aching desire to love again.
My thoughts wonder why you've captured my eye?
This absence you hold hinders this myst'ry.
As time passes it's harder to deny
My strong desire to give you my hearts key.
My thoughts wonder what creature could be you?
For none have I seen as more beautiful!
The luster of you own radiant hue
Shows all I need to keep my heart hopeful.
       Yet all the love I hold for you, I fear
       These troubled times have kept us far from near.

IV.

Fearless faith the guide
Framework of divinity
Awake dormant dreamers
Wisdom's begun

Transcendent dimension
A frequency unknown
Altered minds align
To unite as one

The walls fall
Towards seat of mercy
Surrender reverie
Cape enclosed

Beauty's Visage

His wild inhalation of ebony
Chaste locks and curls, untouched, untaught, untamed.
His aeolian anima aye aching
Aspired release in billow blackened sea.
Her audibly drawn well sets hearts aflame
As sense is form, shaping, shading, shaking.
Her firmament surrounds wept agape claimed.
An eyeless ocean mist of still longing
As mooned lumen, conforms, consoles, conceives.
Such eyes of noon-day's light left man's well lame
Incapable of verbally viewing.
Creations beautiful language does tell,
How man's goddess was formed, how loved so well.

Reality a Mirror

I'm awake in listless sleeplessness,
My subconscious prevents my dreams.
Never sleeping, constant weeping,
Bloodshot eyes, useless highs,
Slay the conscious,
I'm subconscious.

Image in the mirror,
False reality revered,
Enhanced awareness,
Sleeping feared.

Daydream isn't dreaming,
The sound of the wind is seething,
Forget to breathe,
Blind to see.

This world in two dimensions,
Double answers to each question,
What is truth? Who can say,
When two worlds come as they may.

I hibernate the mind to find
The time to realize reality,
Do I live on the outside inferior,
Or in the inner, all superior.

Portrait

Tabula raza canvas
Stained white and waiting
Caressed by the artist arm
Vision-less demeanor met
Shadows whet this visage
Softly whit a sightless gaze
Eyes entombed—
Quickly etched
Shoulders drown—
Wisps curl, flow around
A barren skull, loosely formed
Uttered silent breath engraved
Upon slivered lips of ebony
Ovals of darkness shadowed
From dimpled nostrils flare
Reflected bleached flesh—
Veils guise
Bleak masked—
The hue-less charm
Of this pale-charred portrait
Mimics Libra's innocence
Harbors wingless heaven
Of all color and none
Melt within sphere of clear
Dissipate into nothing
Tabula raza canvas—
Still
Born—

Whisper Wind

Wild wisps cast life
Life upon the dead
Trees forbidden dance
As seasons pass
Carried words echo
From ancient lands
The dust unsettles
A new time's begun

Without sight
Sense reveals past
Unveils truth to life
Zephyr wind upon us
Spirit make us live
Dance and move
Voices in the air
Lost lives unsung

Violent winds howl with me
Unknown winds sing to me
Send word of the wise
Shout taunts for the fool

Underneath my skin
Storms fade
New mist forms
Sickly clouds arise
Parched lips
This harsh wind
An echo of hate
From past mistakes

Let the sands of time stop the wind
Let the hands of fate spin the wheel

Find our hiding place
Whisper to our face
Wind blow in power
Wind blow this season hour
Wild wisp cast life
Without sight
Underneath my skin
A new times begun
Lost lives unsung
An echo of hate
From past mistakes
Whisper wind

Violent winds howl with me
Unknown winds sing to me
Send words of the wise
Shout taunts for the fool

Let the sands of time stop the wind
Let the hands of fate spin the wheel

Find our hiding place
Whisper to our face
Wind blow in power
Wind blow this season hour

Let the sands, let the hands
Wind blow, whisper wind

Let the hands, let the sands
Wind blow, whisper to me

Numina

Her spirits touch does rest upon this man
Unconscious truths unknown—save silent thoughts—
A soul unbound will heed agape's cry
Too haunt the heart akin to natures plan.
An absent song the sea of dreams had brought,
A moaned melody—siren sung awry—
In moonlight raven nights the pain began,
A whispered wail of love now veiled, was wrought
Behind the sightless gaze of formless eyes
Which failed to grasp her bloom—then beauty ran—
To grace a life she sought, while lost he rot,
Condemned too live by truths imagined lies.
   Her spirits kiss will linger on, now wake
   The loveless heart of mans eternal ache.

Silent Song

Everyone, yet no one hears this fervent song,
Sung about weepless willows, a whisper wind,
Wave upon wave caress this sand-less shore,
As endless ages make thoughts evolve forever.
Feeble sighs, countless cries, shore to shallow,
A woven mind, only to release an unread poem.

Far beyond the vast void an adventurous wind
Blows from blanketed cliff to speckled shore,
From rustled leaves to this disturbed shallow,
As words remain amiss in this unheard poem.
Viewless effect measures the wept song
Of one whose soul yearns in torment forever.

Subdued by false pretense thought to be forever,
Still realizations compose the timeless song,
Unlearned ears savor the echo in the wind,
Sung by the cynic whose mind is most shallow.
Anonymity befriends the author of the poem,
Ensuing the footsteps that walk the ebbing shore.

Irrefutably voices utter against the lawless shore,
As earnest cries resound form depths so shallow,
The Muse's gift resides in this misplaced poem,
From the excessive expulsion of purposeless wind.
These eloquent lines to only be suppressed forever,
An urgent message hidden in this lost love song.

Still stale, stagnant, no eyes to read this poem,
This wisdom lost, futile time spent gone forever,
He wished to share the meaning of the silent song,
Yet overlooked by walkers of the distant shore.
Those who heed the calls of troubled wind,
Wind that sores through thoughts so shallow.

Unable to swim deeper, caught in these shallow
Constant waves washing over the unread poem,
A searching soul opens what time delayed forever,
This immortal soul, ocean soul, sings one song.
Released in one, the words written on this shore,
By one, carried throughout the world by the wind.

The careless wind, brings beauty to every shore,
Of the now read poem, able to sore from the shallow,
To be lost in forever, never to cease the souls song.

V.

Divine Intention
Perichoretic possession
Lights solitudal service
Invoked by this wind

Commune within this intuit
Remembered answers to reveal
The writ of ancient ideals
Spiral about inhalation

Muse upon the two-edged
Truth abides amidst
The etheric center
Where peace awaits acceptance

Barrier Blue

Seemingly distant lands split by salty tides,
Fastened once a part of the others shore.
Timeless shifted sands from far beyond
Have shattered the heart mended by love.

Nature had drawn its curtain ocean blue,
Separated two souls from fate's purpose.
All hope now gone to depths of shadows,
The expanse had stole the moment mistaken.

Her beauty too precious to witness by mortal eyes,
Risen above this void of distance long in waiting.
Riding on precarious winds to nestle by her lost,
Along demeanor coy she came with pious poise.

Lifetimes spent exiled, away from beauty's truth,
Only white wings lifted the possible reality to light.
Sphere's time waits while this black beauty rises,
Nevermore be sifted as this heartbeat strays away.

Sought in endless catacombs of loves divinity,
Forever apart, together forever in breaths moments.
Existence timeless, still time melts from the present,
As times pass, another replaces what's never found.

Misty Dawn

Murky clouds
Over icy waters
Water so
Strange
Cold
Deep
Fog surrounds
Lonely
Stone tower
It is
Still
Alone
Staring at the sea
The humming sound
Of the rumbling ocean
On the
Ancient
Sunless
Shore
Here the great dark majesty
Of the deeps has come
His cry akin to the towers'
One of his own
Rushing
Crashing
Breaking the towers
Essence
Solitudes presence
The sun
I, I
I am
Gone

Disturbed Sky

The sun pined past the sea-line of the earth,
Blood red the clouds burned.
Time stood still,
These scarlet flamed eyes, gazed toward heaven.

They lined the sky like slaughtered sheep,
Coats stained, hued deep rose.
I sat upon,
The firmament above the ground

    In a seat of self-reflection.

Polluted skies, the light dispersed.
Counted sheep,
They faded into seeming darkness.
Vivid sleep,
Darkening illusion.

    My ignorant seat forgiven.

"In this time, the sky
I revere.
Good night sweet light,
I'll sleep with you tonight."

Martyr Messenger

The sacred sentinel
Watcher
Of times passed
Loathe too repeat
Future charms
Compelled by malignant
Thoughts
Ill will sought
Human displeasure

The martyr messenger
This black raven
Sheol's spawn
A stricken deliverer

Crooked beak
Bent misshapen
Recoil abrupt harbinger
Dealt through terror
To rule the world
Sent for pain
Doomed to die

The martyr messenger
This black raven
Sheol's spawn
A diseased creature

Unwilling perverse attention
It strays into unguarded thoughts
Brooding unholy fear
Into the eyes of witnessed innocence

She'll hide her face when the raven comes
She'll sing for grace when the raven comes
He'll plead guilty as the raven calls

He'll hail mercy as the raven falls

Forevermore darkness falls
When this raven caws
Turning light to night
The messenger awaits

The martyr messenger
This black raven
Sheol's spawn
An undead Harold

A harlot of lost souls
Pleasure un-divine
A hedonist for ideals
Fatal justice for the animals of
Humankind

The serpents kiss
Wilts the raven feathers
The Holy's hands
Forge the watcher's eye

The martyr messenger
This black raven
Sheol's spawn
An untold myth

Ceases to desist
Mortal in its time
Yet the raven endures death
For death is home

The martyr messenger
This black raven
Sheol's spawn
A demons haven

They'll sleep in silence when the raven sings
They'll dance in deliverance when the raven sings
We'll weep cowed as the raven descends
We'll laugh aloud as the raven ascends

Siren's Sorrow

The song of the Sirens is sung,
Lulling the silent sorrow,
While delaying the morrow.
And with it desperate cries arise,
From this night of passions demise.

This wailing weep of loneliness,
To the men she longs,
Heard as seducing songs.
Still, Fates forsake forbidden desire,
As men doomed, sail the Styx forever.

Alone, she wades the still waters,
The placidity of her soul,
Abandoned the name, immortal.
As each suitor's life is swept away,
Love's vigor is slowly washed away.

The song of the Siren's now sung,
Swallowed by the sea,
This last zealous plea.
Waves of sorrow, now haunt her cries,
From this night of passions demise.

sphere of darkness

mention this ancient day
time circles back again
white light of endless hue
shattered the eternal night
bending darkened dogma

alienated from its first form
sightless white dwells alone
awry away from such darkness
split as time began
separated till this verse stills

solemn black now longs
the lit of morn
but fades from its lost partner
shied from the union broken
mourning now until an end

the shifting shape of tragedy
shed the white from black
breaking the balance of the past
dark now embraces lights path
seeking it before it's passed

their undone flight to find
the one that was cast aside
existing in an endless cycle
of the huntress and the hunted

their loathsome longing
between this invisible expanse
to create a form of one

forever a part of another
bound to find the other

waiting till this sphere of darkness
sheds a warmer light

to force whites heat to night

VI.

Balance
This sphere of darkness
Renounce errant emotion
Silent beauty manifest

Self numbed psyche
Heeds this voids cry
For native revelation
Compassion on all mankind

Scales set to weigh
Agape's appeal
To order this chaos
By the grace of paradise

Awaken the Dreamer

Driven by instincts survival the creature reigns supreme
Allowing base knowledge control beliefs filtered by lies
The domain of negativity entices constant weakening desires
Continual suffering plagues the child of infantile gesture
Silent longing echo's within, revealing mankind's nature
Freedom faintly calls hearts trapped atop death's pyres
The unseen world awaits aloof behind embodied disguise
All answers relate to one within the dream

Spiraling into subconscious slumber, the grand fantasy
The waking hours imaginings brought to vision
Traipsing wanton lust to gut wrenching horror
A chaotic myriad of grandiose illusive constancy
The nightly cycle ever presents arrogant division
Swallowing whole the dreamer, an egoistic whore
Lost amidst the creative, forcing innate inconsistency

Seclusion, the self imagined bodily prison
Its seductive entrance keeps one separate
Belittled mind blind to perceptions poison
Divided world the only unholy schism
Sufferings substitute allows love to interpret
Translation transcends through lights inner prism

Figures function in seeming existence
The players consort with no-thing
Grasping gratitude for self's patience
Minds tongue stilled by everything
Illusion fades in steadfast silence

Light's relevance has grown
Beauty in sights perfection
Truth in errors correction
Prayers deliverance now known

Apparent as witness
Artistry of divinity
Dreamer as awareness

Blessed humanity
Inherent serenity

I

Luciferous

Guised in narcissistic vanity
Alluring an artist
With seldom song so sweet.
Radiant with ambiance
The morning star
In pale moonlit night.
Enchants the mortal soul
With lusts desire
Of vampire visage fair.
An illusion so pure
Naked eye beauty
Such is the angel of light.

Temptress of perfection
Lacked true flaw
Tainted is passions power.
The scholar of Juan
Essence of creation
This mirrored image.
Quenching darkened spirit
With light extinguished
Renowned angel of song.
All man's minds unjust
Condemned by pride
As fallen beauty lies.

The Perfection of the Night

The day is done
Now dusk's begun
Twilight is sinkin'
It's time for thinkin'
Let dreams escape
The subconscious landscape
And mold into
The dimension of you
Dawn now broken
In silence spoken
Morn's light arises
As beauty disguises
And time is lost
No matter the cost
As day now entreats
Such reality depletes
And all is forgiven
As judgment is mis-given
What now is light
The perfection of the night

The Way

Now begins a path of life, willed by hallowed conception,
Conceived through love's continual unfailing persistence.
Benign light reveals the witness of ones sure redemption.

True sight, conveyed by the child's eye of pure innocence.
The world of darkness subtly destroys ones inner clarity;
Stay still, silent and steadfast in the ineffable divine essence.

Realize the heart of mankind holds compassion's infinity
And the mind is freed through constantly willed surrender.
Then love is all pervading, known as one undoes mystery.

As work becomes apparent, remember the way of nature.
Heavenly acts of unity unveil loves unchanging just reward.
Many are the paths, yet the end's eternal, the light's forever.

Bound by the greatness of the Supreme spirit that is Lord,
Amidst the presence of peace placed upon his blessed son,
The world succumbs as reality is revealed by truth's sword.

Now to live the life of childlike faith, too inherit all as one.
Seek within the heart, through silent selfless contemplation.
Divinity complete within and throughout the mind undone,
Certain as the morning sun is the truth of love's salvation.

Plucking Petals

Infinity held her thriving blossom,
While times essence lasts forever,
This island beauty no less immortal,
Her havens beckon this life to come.

Stretching out to soak in the shower,
As "Each drop keeps a precious petal
Of beauty, taken by mortal hearts from
This fragrant hued wild island flower."

Slowly fades timed tears begin to fall,
While the shifted sands call for home,
The dimmed light, the candle quiver,
As enticed signs a future to enthrall.

Her time to flourish, to grow for some,
As island rain calms her silent shiver,
This life to live much more than mortal,
While eternity holds her thriving blossom.

Sanctuary

One's amidst the Sanctuary

Again the journey's taken
Along the path now gone
When it began all was forgotten
Forever none will die ever
From the light one has come

Walk among your kinsmen
Adhere to nature's will
Be silent, be still
Know that all are chosen
Now realize the peace
Let the body-mind decease

Sound hallowed heard all around
Screams released by the supreme
Known within as is one's own
Sacred grounds tread by the dead
Sung's the song what has begun

This haven's evolution
Beyond reason
The forest green
Forever unseen
It dissipates into a memory

Awake the soul's at stake
Capture the moment of rapture
Sense one wills purpose immense
Mind in trance contemplates the blind
Free to just be never the need to see

Guardians of timeless nature
Grow creation all around
Mans hand delays the inevitable

The seeds of life cannot be strangled
Beauty unhindered
To live is life
Silent
Still
In the Sanctuary

VII.

Ephenathicism
Just in its reason's voice
Of solemn serenity
To stabilize understanding

Followed Way to Natures
Immortal placidity
Dwelt within the Muses well
Wisdom lies in times stead

Foundational instinct
Based upon inner desire
Too shed the skin
Grasping wills holy instant

The Consumer

The flame sustains heats adaptation
As all that burns transforms
Fueled by life's sustenance
While shades of gray collide with clarity
Pure becomes as essence pervades
And ashen embers now remain
To endure the drawn out death
Once progressed

As truth begins all else fades
Fire the freedom released of pain
Now peace transcends no-mind
Impartial the witness observes
Akin and on to all that is
Hallowed glimpses of light
Uniting all within the soul
Consumer consumed

Wait Awhile

Close your eyes and wait awhile,
Wait for me to reappear.
Close your eyes and search your dreams,
See me smile, release your fear.

Inside your heart, my arms wide wait,
They wait for you.
My arms wait for your embrace,
I am the moments, as they pass by.

Still I wait, wait for you,
Open your eyes and search my smile,
Feel this passion, my fearless love,
Open your eyes and stay awhile.

Whirling Wed

Enthralled amidst alluring twilight's eyes,
She clasped his hands, now shifting for her thighs,
The Muse's music molds l'amour as one,
Their souls entranced, the dance had just begun.
Now steps align behind the whirling wed
As shadows mirror paths unknown they tread,
Into the night of whitening unlight,
They spiral deeper down as wings take flight.
So lost amidst their psyches united form
As astral sight of thirds this swirling storm,
Uplifting winds ridden by spirits saved,
In circular advance beyond the grave.
      The dance constant as pure as light allows
      As one they found the key to heaven now.

While We Weep

While agony resounds from the Banshee's lips
And sorrow wails from the Siren's lungs,
Deaths echo longs for its songs sung
As lured minds sail to seek love in sinking ships.

While distant gloomy skies slink to dry grounds
And transparent droplets seek new form,
Sketches divinely draw a darkening storm
As lidless beads of a sightless expanse abound.

While glacier crevasses crumble into the sea
And drifts dive down mountainsides,
Ice's nature becomes one with the tide
As disturbed dunes of peaks in terror flee.

While dusk's light leaps atop the forest's masts
And bleak nights touch upon white water,
Earth's star pulls its linear reach tauter
As rippled rivers repeat tears of nights past.

Esanem

Recoil the tensioned thrust
As bonds bound the bottom
To a steel-stained altar
Wrists in shackles ankles
Wrought in chains
Released domain to the will
Of another's hands
Manipulate
Ones desire to
Copulate
Discreet sustenance flowing
Through valves bled in return
To pumping viscera
In submission
On the floor of threshing
Under towering top
Tippled in ecstasy
As one prey's n plays
Over sweetness of thirst
Quenched from the nape
So succulent
Scarlet tainted lips poured
Down parched deserved throat
As erect pores rigidly perspire
Awaiting the never release
Taunt from feathered lace
Beaded leather break sheathed
Flowered petals blooming
Blood red
Spinal tapped
Nervous veins ebbing arteries
Forced forming fleshly roses
Painful pleasure mingle
In imperfect beauty of
Aphrodite's design
Vessels shifting from

The Eros divines
Masked seducer fulfilling
Agony's request
To sense punishing
Reward
Once peak of pleasure once
Found vaginismus erupts
Within convulsion contorts
Salty-lidded stinging rings
Curved lips laughing weep
Shivered sense creeping beads
Along dewed white-red
Bodied blood induced being
Harmonic breath
Short of sighed acceptance
Uttered silent gratitude
Entangled draping twilight's
Stripes damped from porous
Pressure
Clenching in wait
Requiring pulsated presence
Plunging to fill the void
So swollen
Limbs released
Red ringed memories bind
What's left behind
Waterfalls white-watered
Avalanches cascading
As time ceases increases
Slowing accentuating
Realities fading existence
A loss of air
Pained pleasure peaks possibility
Fettled faint
Awake skin to skin
Enclasped as one
Knowing the need to bleed
Lying atop steel-stained altar

The threshold of wisdom
The sadist's seduced
The plea requited
The top bottomed

Mantled Mystic

Mantled mystic,
Emerge spirit winged.
Vanishing essence of embodiment,
Veracity immersed the expanding existence
Reaching beyond heavens grasp to realize
Re-occurrences continual, reveal untouched invisible realms unified.
Mystified mind unravels reality timelessly returned.
Discovered aspirant completes orbited conscious.
Liberty uncaged stimulates non-being,
Dissolving sensations spurious.
Inheritance redeemed
Absolution.
Redeemed inheritance,
Spurious sensations dissolving.
Non-being stimulates uncaged liberty,
Conscious orbited completes aspirant discovered,
Returned timelessly reality unravels mind mystified.
Unified realms, invisible, untouched, reveal continual re-occurrences.
Realize, to grasp heavens beyond reaching.
Existence expanding the immersed veracity.
Embodiment of essence vanishing,
Winged spirit emerge,
Mystic mantled.

VIII.

Veritasophia
Embrace flesh inflamed
Purging progression
Doused soul in spirit fire

Absolute atonement
Hopes deliverance
Layers veiled lifted
Reality formless

Smoldering within
Purified gold
All is known
In visions perfection

This Eternal Visit

She has yearned and wept for the certainty of a close
companion,
He has woven the design of subtle seeds within a searching
soul,
Her eyes of awed innocence betray the years of broken
attachments,
His solitary ignorance of beauty has delayed this inevitable
union.

Life's exchange of perspectives has revealed itself whole,
This experience enhances loves never-ending advancements.
Her heart of infinite grace has found it's communion,
His divine demeanor ever now joined with its equal.

A beautiful occasion brought these two spirits to
commitment,
Most blessed by fervent prayer and timeless determination.
Now to set these two lovers of heavens favor into holy free-
fall,
May their lives be one of shared long-lived joyous
monuments.

The intimacy you'll share will take you to where God reveals
his essence,
Together your lives will be touched by God's powerful still
presence.
Your union holy, your love completely, your vows truly, your
beauty exquisite.
As one now undone and formless may all bless and honor
this eternal visit.

My Valentine

In sleepless slumber she dreams of me,
Her minds' thoughts align with mine,
On this day she, will be my valentine,
Speechless held with no words to speak, but poetry.

If she gives consent, I'll give a kiss,
For her heart for forever becomes eternal,
My love penetrates touch, it grows deeply internal,
If love be blind, then love be truly bliss.

I'd cradle her to peaceful sleep,
If she'd be mine this lovers night,
To awake, in her dazed gaze in the dawns' light,
Her first night of real rest, she began to weep.

This day of love is meant to entice
The union between two lovers minds,
To grow more intimate until they find,
That the power of love will always suffice.

So, if this woman will be mine,
If she'll lay down her sorrow and concede,
I'll give her all the love she'll ever need,
If you see my love as true, will you be my valentine?

Relentless

Times fervent fickle changing
Occurs without relent.
Troubles arise and keep bombarding,
Can't arrest the constant aching.
You feel that hurt is heaven sent.

Excessive experience has made you grow,
Verbal poison caused you pain.
Broken relationships have let you go,
Into hell so you could know
The suffering of sins' stain.

Still the wounds, muster fear,
Through every turn you're left to learn,
Without God, tears well near,
And only hate looks through the mirror.
Discard the shadow that's made you mourn.

Love conquers hates hold,
It releases raped innocence,
Carves peace in the soul.
Until baked bread turns to mold,
Delayed is loves deliverance.

When found, pain passes,
Relieved pressure pounding ceases.
Lordly love encompasses,
Deep within, it possesses.
Then hates hold is ripped to pieces.

Taken

Behavior betrayed by a body not your own
Mentation meaningless within your mind
Your being taken
 Away
From yourself
In sequential surrender you succumb
An apparition alienated from your soul
Your being broken
 Away
From yourself
The failing fear awaits about your demise
As darkness depletes leaving your fearless
Your being awoken
 Away
From yourself
Gifts given graciously long your embrace
The howling heart hearkens your inner ear
You've been taken
 Within
The Self
Total truth tugs gently at your essence
Uncovered unconscious now you weep
You've been broken
 Within
The Self
Light lavishly lives among your being
Eyeless aether eases your enlightenment
You've been awoken
 Within
The Self

Magus Incarnate

An oaken limb grafts the Magus incarnate
And light cloaks this clairvoyant sentient.
Steadfastly beats the crestfallen heart
Where within, awaits the watcher of its gate.

Wizardly aura amidst depths now diffident,
Behind shadows darkness delved an art,
Still stalled until the weeper meditates,
Upon the spiritless throne, the king laments.

The mantled monarch's magic does impart
As slumbering soul awakens prostrate
Before sovereign solitude, minds consent
To reveal the signet of ones counterpart.

Wisdom written, etched staff, wielded adeptly,
Eliminates illusive entities of destruction.
The crown ascends beyond planes so subtly,
Into unconscious center circling in completion.

Formless Souls

She sought the haven loves essence surrounds,
She sought the source of love's deliverance,
And found the fervor placed within this man,
Impassioned fire, a flame set free unbound.
He reached for love to furnish fate's advance,
He reached for heaven's face to grant this plan,
Enthralled by beauty now his princess crowned,
Enchanted forever in her romance.
They share the visage grasped as love began,
They share the honest virtue love has found,
To live amidst intimacies entrance,
United life to live in Heaven's hands.
       Incomplete forms entrapped inside their bond,
       Grow formless love as two souls correspond.

IX.

Ecstasy of the Saint
Peacefulness of the Still
Purusha of the Sage
Infinity of the Self

Allness
Sustained by grace
Surpassed by karma
Potential boundless

Exist as always
Way of the heart
Way of the mind
Reveal the crown

Living Wisdom Well

Oh, beauty's truth enticed so well,
With slow intent caressed her beading skin,
Impassioned utterance from ev'ry sense within.
Convulsing curved her spine, she fell
To weakened fleshly desires; yearningly
Awaits her lover, compelled by her mystery.
In moments stillness there they dwell,
In coitus contemplation as wisdom
Unveiled reveals its beautiful firm axiom.

It comes as desp'rate Harlot's cries,
To deafened ears and narrow-minded skulls;
Accept her counsel; listen to her song that lulls.
Delight in lust did Wise Man's eyes,
His legion harem justified his view
That frequent conscious drawing woman's wells was due.
While savage Enkidu now lies
With Fortune's gates surrounding potent drive,
Unkempt emotion calmed will make wisdom revive.

This Holy Chalice supped so deep
With milky crystalline reflux his tope,
Now tippled under wisdom's constant grinding grope.
The Muse's draft, this well they keep,
Their arts contrived on knowledge keenly caught,
And pure the dark abyss where purged belief's are sought.
A mirrored moonlit beauty weeps
As ecstasy transforms her weak desire,
This placid picture pleasure made her nerves form fire.

A secret hidden long by light,
This truth too shrouded under heaven's hands,
As desperation rises, freely burns its brand.
From Living waters drank this night,
A Godly wisdom drawn from wells of life,
A spirits haven, willed to copulate its wife.

Her hair so black and long rare sight
About his caked rough feet she washed with tears,
And welled within her master's eyes, her wisdom hears.

Promised Death

Being dragged through rough trampled streets,
　　　Beaten by whips and scorned by laughter.
Open wounds festering on a blood broken back.
　　　Walking, waiting, stumbling, just wanting to end.
Weeping, shouting, laughing seems all I hear,
　　　Still, peace, surrounding me, no need to fear.
I felt the kiss, the time had come, the end so near;
　　　My father turned away, many reasons he can't stay.
Closer and closer still, I can see my destiny,
　　　For humanities impossibility on that tree I'll to my
rest.
My robed ripped off, cast for petty sacred lots.
　　　My love grows stronger still as burdens grow heavier.
Pain flows through my veins and up my spine,
　　　Cold steel driven through, mockingly takes its time.
Dull spikes hang me now, a crimson-crown of thorns on my
brow.
　　　My breathing strained, lungs stretched out complain.
But a love grows deeper, grace flowing freer,
　　　I can endure, my time as come, now this will be done.
They don't know or understand, my death has paid the price,
　　　From know, till an end, this day will be told, the
victory won.

The Raven Calls, The Siren Sings

The Raven calls, the Siren sings,
Bewitching these rapacious signs.
Amidst these vivid empyrean dreams,
Lost love clings to redundant things.

These euphonic songs, so benign,
Release the pain or so it seems.
Stillness in feeling, the Siren brings,
Her alluring finds the longing mind.

Her muted songs, smothered screams,
Heeded by countless "prince charmings".
Their ravenous thoughts set to malign,
Innocence they ream, corrupt her dreams.

This Raven cries, it's lost its wings,
Bound to thoughts and impassioned signs.
Her formless soul it must redeem,
Enticed by things the sweet Siren sings.

Perilous Beauty

Instants of truth de-mask forms mystery,
Revealing the wonder of what once was unknown.
The hearts purpose rising beyond instinctual grounds,
Within the center of light all unfolds
And the vastness that is love receives ones beauty.

Visions of wo-man as one arose all alone,
Eyes so radiant seared the heart unbound,
A visage hidden behind a mask of spiraling holds
The esoteric wonder of what must be free.
Her yearning for healing in an instant shown.

The sight now aware of the garment around
This being; a shroud of mist enfolds
A formless essence apparent as perilous beauty.
So alive the witness allows the darkness to atone,
For truth in its simplistic surrender is found.

As one's consciousness arises more meaning is foretold.
Lying atop her breasts of pearl, a piece of jewelry
Lay, which illuminates the soul no one owns.
A seeming ruby of enlightening that surrounds
All being; her bosom within knows loves mould.

Worn on the brow, a golden crown one sees,
Now rays of holiness undo fears groan,
As she abides in paradise where songs of joy resound.
The highest courts graced by a presence untold,
For what is spoken is lost in mannors memory.

Now the separateness of loss redeemed by truth
First bewilders then releases the mind of reason,
As her persona of perfection is realized.
The pilgrim now is the vision it always knew,
While one may voice suggestion, she, is eternally you.

Aeon Soul of Golden Dawn

Daughter of the angelic child, adorned and abandoned to
watch and wait.
Mother of the bene elohim, provider and protector to spirit
and sentience.
The gemstone of ages, the breathing cornerstone, the aeon
soul of golden dawn.
The final episodes, moments of reality, clarifying the
progression to peace.
This solemn sound mind in steadfast holiness shares the
honest hearts cry.

Fetus of the Tear

Mangled within a weeping womb,
Manifest horror a hallowed haven.
Dirge wails of a teardrop tomb,
Damned hails of a rapacious raven.
Evade incision of the holiest hole,
Echo innocence of the stillborn soul.

Amidst this sphere of darkness,
Purpose left too soon undone,
Attained purity in stillness,
The light and death of one,
Hastens cycle of lifelessness.

Drown now down trails of tears,
Halted floodgates withdraw flow,
Too within births fervent glow.
Years compress this all now clear.

Conscious spirit meld truth of thirds,
Child's self sight enlightenment.
The will distilled heals heaven's word,
Deaths demise lies in torment,
As intimacies internal awareness heard.

Escape illusion of the embodied embryo,
Enliven intuition of the spirituous spore.
Deemed radiant with a glorious glow,
Dawn broken with a silent score.
Mother rejoice your revelation received,
Mercy crowned your child conceived.

X.

Deafened ears take heed
Muted mouths serve silence
Blinded eyes illumine vision
Bodiless touch observe sense

Clouds dispersed
Miracles radiant
Blessings limitless
Unmanifest ineffable

Transfigured perspective
Hallowed ascension
Heavens aspirant
Wholly receiving

The Dance of One

Such light illumines timeless nature,
Ambient flows woven in purposeful design,
Rays so potent disperse darkness divine.
Radiant glowing embers linger demur,
A terrible light that unfolds under invisible fire,
Awaiting its partner to envelope its dark desire,
                Too dance.
Such nothingness forms a distant void,
So dark dreary dense is its quenched core,
This hole in space where gravity tore,
Nature's murderer loathed blackness destroyed.
This viewless void welcomes its willing companion,
Accompanied itself together inside the illusion,
                They dance.
Such time expands the edges of eternity,
Bound to follow the law of one,
In this spherical forever it waits undone,
Through the dimension doors lies the key.
Seconds lapse in times slow waned decay,
Within this ring unending death does prey,
                To Dance.
Such space estranges the enmity of emptiness,
Its notion to dwell in the time allowed,
Constant motion—moved matter—screams aloud,
The entropy of the age induces changes distress.
Hand in hand time takes the lead as space concedes,
Bound in random repetition the eternal leads,
                The dance.
Such corporeal reality lingering beyond humanities hold,
Ever illusions confusion disrupting the souls reason,
Havens of the spirit still many minds treason,
Infused inside knowledge of the truth known never told.
Burdening the unseen with unwilling desire to feel,
Exiling the seat of this sacred temple to reveal,
                This dance.

Such subsistent beings formed bodily into existence,
Man's tool to prey for reign above what's unknown,
Using fleshly virtues to discover the will of one,
Struggling to deny the intimate soul's resistance.
Through the webbed wheel of spirit's dimensions,
They circle in on one in flesh suit unison,
                    To dance,
              The dance of one.

Intoxicate

Silly secreted sadness,
Suffocates such seemingly sauntering supreme states,
Seeking sublime serenity.
The teetering times taunt tangled teaching's truths.
Taken through tough trials,
Turning towards thorough tedious
Awakenings.
Abrupt and abundant,
Adhering all anima always
Around awareness,
Astonished to see Itself.

And then,
The solitude of the multitudes blanketed the sky,
Like the first falling of crystal life,
And all alive fell silent within itself
As if asleep or dreaming.
From one instant of remembrance,
Life as it is brought about the shift inside,
All that's left is to accept the inevitable,
Be vulnerable and know, you are truly alive.

Astral Fantasia

Torment lied dormant inside his weary soul
As the sea sprayed ceaselessly.
Whitewashed grains sparkled in twilight's light.
Silent nature,
Sprawled out in consternation, contemplating
The numina desire.
Peering through—
Silk-milky night—
At full moons reflected rainbow bending
To his sea-stained eyes.
A wind ridden song, ebbing closer with the tide
Full of impassioned instincts bloom.
This lustrous plea, twitched an echo
Within.
Singing sung song
She idled amidst shallow seas—
Edge of life and song drown—
Wading, dancing, wave by wave.
Faery soul,
Seeking about chaos for delayed spirits touch.
Streams of mist wash the night sky
Awaiting sparkled starlit shine,
Now align to from in purposeful design.
The song of the sought,
Lullaby divine.
Seas lagoon captured moonlit shore
With he waiting there fixed on suns sons
Encircled twilit night.
Darkness entombed the two,
On this summers solstice, earth's mid-drifts treasure.
Underneath their spherical shelter,
An intimate embrace
Of two lost lovers' warm breezed flow.
The waxing wind grew in spirit strength,
Rushing, pushing, rising these love
Fearing souls.

Illumined form within taken from earthly shells
Face to face on astral planes.
In the subconscious firmament
Passionate infatuation reigned as two lovers
Shared beauty's gift of life.
To mimic the flesh
Two spirits, enjoined as one, beneath, among the eyes...

Sea of Dreams

Beneath the sea, this adventure begins.
Traveled the reef, seen the great white.
Beyond the surface all is alive.
Lost are the thoughts of a million men,
Cracked timber, rotting skulls make their den.

Over rocks and through the sea, treasure is found.
Forgotten fortunes, not remembered by ancient men.
The king of the sea, still unknown.
The Oneironaut wanders always until an end.
Dust glitters beneath, secrets hidden 'round every bend.

So vastly measured, portraying impressive purpose.
Species of creation represent the beauty of the blue.
On every shore, strewn in every cove is the age of the seas.
Life is a challenge, death awaits yearning to devour.
Is this a dream, is this the hour.

Piercing eyes, inspect my seeking soul.
Like a constant wave are my weaknesses revealed.
Drowning, choking under all pressures.
Loving hands have gripped my arm,
In this sea of dreams I'm released from harm.

I

Inconspicuous insanity intrudes illicitly in individuality,
It instigates Id's insufferable intellectual infatuation
Inside improvised illusion intolerably ignorant.

Ideals inescapable, instead invoke inward intuition
Illuminating indescribable invitations instant,
Involving I's inaudible interpreted infinity.

Infinite ideologies intertwine ineffably inherent,
Inducing illogical idyllic inverse integrity
Insuring innocence inspired intention.

I invades involuntarily into immortal infancy,
Indwelling internal impartial intimacy.

Meadow on the Edge

The grinning cheshire leopard laughs and giggles with no
relent,
Charmed by Eros she sets the dwindling hearts of man
ablaze.
Instinctual innocence bubbles from her inner circle realms of
sentience.
Surreally sincere she draws the seeker to her distinct
sensuous scent,
Revealing vast caverns of countless adventures and never-
ending days.
A wandering woman traversing lines of thoughts and images
immense,
Creating visions and visual experience to expand and
contract all.

The faerie princess of the enchanted sanctuary, dances with
glee.
Her beauty's essence an amber autumn glow, as forest leaves
in splendor.
Luminous as the sun rays of love, reaches out and envelopes
all mankind.
Eyes of sparkling starry night induce a wondrous willing
reality.
The ten Muses inspire her creative power of inherent artistic
nature.
She sows souls joy within the hearts of heavens beloved
blind.
A vessel of liquid fire that burns through the blood, body and
all.

The meadow on the edge of madness and magic, truth shines
beyond,
Within the groves of the mind, the embrace and warmth of
the mother.
She invokes the insight of Gaia, with wisdom and clear
vision.

The bright playful light of being dwells within her twinkling
diamond,
Releasing vibrant, infinite hues of gold, scarlet and ocean to
others.
Her abundance of love overflows and extends from internal
intension.
The image and intimate of her Self, seeds joy and life in
people all.

The lustrous divine surrounds this visage heaven sent,
An aura of awakening overflows for those that see,
She found a companion graced by this love bond,
To free each beloved who hears her silent call.

XI.

Humors splendor
Dismisses absurdities
Of ignorant perception
Once believed

The child plays
As universes concede
To freedoms dance
Of one will

Collective
Everything as Is
Consciously
Complete as Self

Egregorial Annunciation

Evolve did the wild flower, as springs dawn sprinkled upon
its blooming petals of heavenly hue.
Gentle breeze brushes by, as the sunlight's benign rays
blanket forested valley's beauty below.
Ravished leaves, abandoned by branches, circle to the
ground of seasoned rest to enrich life's flow.
Exquisite shapes in frozen design silently cover the earth,
glowing in an ambiance known by few.

Grave slumber in the womb of splendor the unborn begins
extension in seconds of bliss.
Oscillating patterns gradual collapse as inner solitude
traverses the planes of existence.
Relinquished authority of illusions veil releases the mind
once wandering hells abyss.

Indifferent delusion decimates the swallowed whole soul in
fetal form of depressions despair.
Atrophied senses gripped in constant fluctuating fear,
oppress the stricken seeker in terror.
Latent acceptance of truth tangled in tangible value,
awakened to the wisdom of evermore.
All encompassing ecstasy of the divine state lavishly looses
love upon the mind aware.

Nullified within the whispered wind, perichoretic possession
personifies the etheric center.
Numbed psyche in crystal clear glacial purity, balances this
sphere of celestial clarity.
Unlight overwhelms the still stone of solemn serenity,
relentlessly resonating with vitality.
Naivety's purging progression in visions perfection
consumes the absolute atonement altar.

Collective unconscious memories' dominance, no-thing
remains of reflections indulgence.

Internal integrity instigates immortal infancy, intention indwells instant impartial intimacy.
Absurd fancies of fortunes enigmatic suspense, fill the thought thinker with nonsense.

Today, I, contemplate the observation, of the many myriads of blessed life's crossroads.
Inner divine light reveals the purpose of true prayer's gift that expands and contracts.
Only in enlightening rest will the abundance of peace in heavens kingdom contact.
Nameless is Oneness, Realized in Silence, Become the Truth, these, the final episodes.

Seven Ravens

Greeted by impressive creative forces displayed at the
enchanted entrance.
Seven Ravens scrawled above a magical moon shining in a
solitary forest.
A walled gateway of evergreen arches over the wanderer
entering in silence.

Abstract abodes, erected primevally evolving, lined the path
seldom sought.
Life-giving gardens, balance beautiful growth, governed by
selfless keepers.
Following faery trails, prickled-tickled by leaves extending
wondrous thought.

Trekking through natures nursery of enriching energies
flowing flawlessly.
Gazed upon groves glorious, pondering pools of lovely forest
essence.
Arrival amidst a sanctuary secluded, solid foundation,
forever securely.

An arbutus labyrinth entangles the awakening summit of the
spiral paths dais.
Dragonfly's dart in ways mysterious, wolfish grins gratified
in submission.
Faces smiling soundly, laughter erupts echoes through
kaleidoscope eyes.

This dream-scape bedrock of growing rose quartz ever
coalescing starstruck souls.
Merry the wilderness of ravens domain, swaying silhouette's
in a moonlit mangrove.
Friends follow karma's benevolent destiny, arising from flesh
forming spirits whole.

The wanderer of ancient writ lends wisdom to scribe in the mind of ways witness.
Love the land, live from the land, share the land, all united, this simplicity.
Blessed unfathomably by nature's courtship, attuned to hear the soundless.

This evolving creation building bonds in unbreakable eternal power.
The egregore extending through sphere's upon endless sphere's.
Here in gratitude the being sends serenity in a celestial shower.

Unifying Night

Among the rural murmur, a bedazzled crowd;
Had manifest amidst the expectant glowing eyes
A luminous goddess, the source of beauty's light.
Entranced the isle, advanced in a hov'ring cloud.

Ever closing an eternal gap where two unify,
Along the petal strewn plane rose an awing sight,
An illuminating scene to make high kings proud,
She levitated forward through the ominous sigh.

On the pedestal to bind herself dressed in white,
She took the hand of the man who bowed,
An intolerable sensation encompassed the sky
As these joined souls gave a holy kiss that night.

An eternity to spend together as love allowed,
Sealed by similar stone bands, symbols to rely
On a love made complete while two souls delight,
Forever to live in love under a heavenly shroud.

Sorrowful Wanderer

A spiraling vertigo down depths to despair
A darkness clear envelops souls abyss.
Seek the labyrinth of nothing known
As a familiar song, echoes from lost lair.
A-maze of ends still sought center amiss,
Whisp'ring mis-lead silent mayhem moan.
Eternity's remnants hearken wanderer fair,
Brought the birth of hallowed ancients kiss.
Realigned paths trodden, sorrows savior shown,
Gentle presence consumed the spirit now heir.
Where first began amidst all-none is bliss.
A sphere of consciousness sat the throne.
Within this still life, ambassador of peace
Now reign, the heart suffering cease.
An eternal solace, a duality unified,
Envelops one where blessings collide.

The Truth Within

That fragrant innocence, sweet ignorance
Of natures nurtured souls naivety.
Unspoilt, now surfacing of sightless eyes
Awake allow nothingness too advance
Your sphere's of sententious serenity—
Arise ancestral clarity...arise.
Your beading choices form deliverance
From conscious darkness, bursts tranquil beauty.
Such seemingly unsought awareness cries
Beyond these stricken senses brilliance,
Enveloped within truths unknown frailty
There lies a thund'rous moment realized.
       Unborn of mind, the ancients come to find,
       A spirit left behind, all-one now bind.

All Is One

Memoirs, constructs consciously form past's legion of linear
limited memories.
Illusions of perception plague the embodied believer,
allowing nothings reverence.
Shadow's shroud wrapped around the psyche's felled
mindless condemned seclusion.
Vicious intent, id's blind desecration obscures wills hallowed
altar awareness.
Sight distorted shivers foundations de-based by fearful
unknown spirits lair.
Martyred mind now undone, visions instant reveals Self's
holiness
one.
Peace's abundance dwells amidst raven wings upon cape
encompassed throne.
Gate of immortality opened now agony's steps unveil death
denied.
The masquerade unmasked as presence divine purely
clarifies continuous circle.
Truth's reality conveys totalities reason beyond proof's
ability to comprehend.
Eternal union wholly claimed, the blessed son's inheritance
finally claimed.
All-One

XII.

The Egregore
Eternity's entreaty
Times death
Fathomless unity

Cyclic nature unfolds
As separation ceases
All knees bow
In reverent unison

The glorious song
Now is sung
Remembrance Day
God as One

EPILOGUE

Siedo-en

The tree of ages forever growing...

The seedling settles into the ashen nest, through a fertile faerie fyre's blessing.
Gently suckling at mothers nutrients now sprouting penetrating tails, to revive the stillborn one.
This awakening silent sheltered fetus finds the warmth and lifesblood of sublime consecration.
Its mouth cries out in wonder wriggling with growth and finds heaven's tears softly caressing.

This benevolent beginning a flirtatious movement into being, awoke in the misty morn sun.
Reaching, bending, branching ever higher towards the light, deep rooted in a trusted foundation.
Stalks midst thickening, life's source flowing, light's love absorbing, the sapling now sleeping.
A peace serene, the endearing path spiraling through all changes to become unconditionally undone.

A desperate deliverance, a choice plantation, a miraculous opportunity, an evolving creation.
An encompassing tree of ages of ancestral spirits wisdom, wrought of the life-giving well-spring.
Dancing with zealous Zephyrus to form it's deliberate design, affirming it's solid cornerstone.
An amber ambrosia coursing through it's veins, the universal heartbeat breathes in perfect repetition.

This celestial canopy connects effortlessly to its counterparts, linking root, branch and flower.
In complete co-existence this unified entity covers its beloved in a blanket of blooming power.

As the faerie tale unfolds, as each chapter has ended, the tree will grow on and on into eternity.
A never-ending tale of the ultimate union between two lovers loving all with overflowing ferocity.

The animal totems living within...

The spotted specter slumbers silently secluded among the treetops of the canopies playground.
Its playful tail and serenading eyes secures its mercy seat invisible to all and any seeking being.
The memorable magnificent mane of kingly descent rests reclusive atop the flying water outpost.
Its observing eyes and tempered tail deciphers the desires of all and any creatures around.

Winter shades disguise the timberland denizen as it stalks silently through the fallen forest glistening.
A gleeful grin ere the hunt now howls fervently echoing in the full moonlit night like a distant ghost.
Rushing rivers and buzzing bees call the warm mother of hibernation to cull her cubs to the sounds.
Her graceful guidance gently rears the accepting aspirants with hearing hearts always listening.

She, the iris of Ra, a purified gold inferno of fyre that sparks ablaze all who gaze upon the host.
Once witnessed in true sight, to ash and egg she lies till another sparks alight the fertile ground.
He, the astral Oneironaut, an ebony winged sentinel of silence caws victory evanescent-ling.
Once heard in sought answer, its brothers knowing, the night is governed from mount to coast.

Such an anima relinquished, returns karmically coy, revolving in an ever spiraling oneness.
This deemed gallant gene genius corresponds completely to its companions openness.

Such an animus radiated, digs deeply pious, flamboyantly
transcending space and time.
This grinning delicious desired goddess gives graciously to
its revealing voluptuous rhyme.

The vessel balancing energies divine...

A being knit intricately by the wisest weaver, minuscule
molecules placed with precise intent.
A figure did develop fortunate and whole, infused with a
blessed consciousness aptly aimed.
A vessel verified, stamped with a holy signet, now awakened
from satisfied silence.
A newborn babe, playful and willful, sent to the world to join
the wave of spiritual ascent.

Alone amidst many minds, the child of wonder witnesses the
kaleidoscope of beings named.
Beguiled and bewildered by the cyclone of circumstance the
innocent adapts to bombarding influence.
The tranquil transfer of knowledge, delivers, understanding
to the transparent, natures coincident.
Within the revolving entrance of ever unfolding moments
ones mind is forevermore custom framed.

An emerald throne room of elegance and abundance seats the
epicenter of ones true essence.
Hovering just above and behind the lustrous majestic throne,
the pulse of love shines radiant.
The palpitating power of the healed whole heart resounds
with the living love now claimed.
An inexpressible sensation stills the mind when glowing fyre
flows in an increasing immense.

This life force full of liquid changeable, responds
immediately to its environments consciousness.
The converse of the universe lies inside one and everyone
sharing constantly its luminescence.

This spirit enters the minds united by the grace and gratitude of surrendering devotees.
The committed hearts enjoin in body and mind as they accept the awakening aura of loves refugees.

The life living for all eternity...

The laughing kin mimics of all that's alive, compose relentless giggles truly insurmountable.
Spontaneous outbursts uncontrollable relieve the tension of tedious toiling day after glorious day.
The cachinnating companions writhe in ecstasy on an altar of rose petals and beading perspiration.
Wondering how this ludicrous life can be experienced without release in joyous gesture ineffable.

Aglow, twinning twilight phosphorescent, a starstruck sky, dancing aurora borealis, an isles inlet bay.
Robust autumn moon, the rainbow halo extending, faerie glimpses flash, a forests faultless vision.
Ablaze, spinning spirals incandescent, an empyreal azure, fluttering butterflies beautiful, burns healable.
Glistening spring sun, solar flares absorbing, angel wings soar, a meadows memory shows the way.

The affinity between two whole souls undone creates an undying love unmovable in compassion.
To express this feeling, no words comprehend, the sense numb, the mind utterly unimaginable.
Soothing soil nurtures the growth of the erotic exotic budding blossom, tended to by the magic Faye.
The thousand petaled yab-yum lotus of love unfolds in perfect balance, the yin-yang in breath unison.

This hallowed instant of eternal commitment brings the profound awareness of love beyond life.
This moment binding beauty with beauty, love with love, humble husband with wondrous wife.

A miraculous day of blessings divine, joyful smiles, tales to tell and memories granted by grace.
Lights source shines the brightest within when two become one for an eternity of loves embrace.

The marriage complete, the journey begins...